DINO HUNT

DINO HUNT
This book belongs to:

_____

Jonathan. I dedicate this book to you, son. You already know everything there is to know about dinosaurs, so here's a book just for fun. I hope you like the pictures and poems, and this book gives you the same passion for reading that you already have for dinosaurs.

Love you,

Dad

DINO HUNT

My name is Jonathan.
My parents are cavemen.
Off I go today.
No time to stop and play
'cause I've got dinosaurs to slay!
Here's my favorite song to grunt,
before a dino hunt:
"Dilly, Dally, Dino.
Hear what is true—
I'm on a hunt for you!
Jab! Stab! Grab!
When I grow a little older,
smash you with a boulder,
take you home on my shoulder!
Feast, feast, feast,
on a giant beast.
Bigger, Bagger, Binder,
where can I find her?
Dilly, Dally, Dino-saur!"

VELOCIRAPTOR

I'd like to be the captor,
of this female dino-raptor.
Really would've trapped her,
if she wasn't so much faster.
Racing through jungle grass—
how long will I last?!
I'm feeling pretty gassed.
Running, running, running,
faster, faster, faster.
As brave as I can be,
had to flee up a tree.
I'll jump for joy and glee,
if she doesn't eat me!

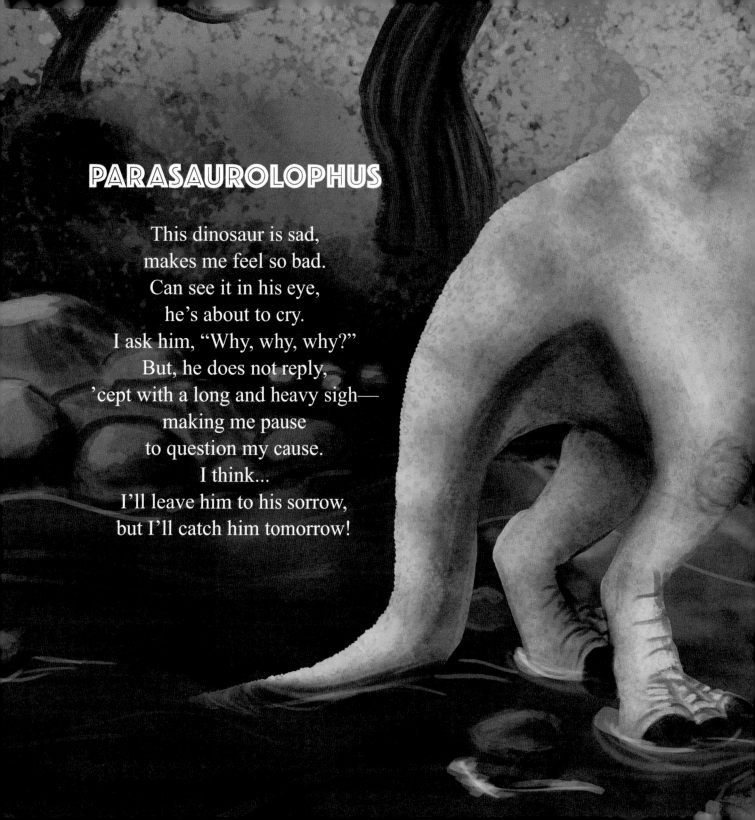

PARASAUROLOPHUS

This dinosaur is sad,
makes me feel so bad.
Can see it in his eye,
he's about to cry.
I ask him, "Why, why, why?"
But, he does not reply,
'cept with a long and heavy sigh—
making me pause
to question my cause.
I think...
I'll leave him to his sorrow,
but I'll catch him tomorrow!

MOSASAURUS

This dino is so fishy,
but not quite a fish.
If it could only walk,
it would be a croc!
It gave me a stare,
and growled like a bear,
"Come closer if you dare."
I really do swear,
my courage did flare!
I nearly charged in there!
But then I really didn't care,
'cause a scaly crocofish,
wouldn't be my momma's wish
for a tasty dinner dish.

ELASMOSAURUS

This dinosaur is in the sea,
so far away from me
that she is hard to see.
I have no raft to row,
no sailboat wind can blow,
so, I already know,
the chase would be too slow.
I better let her go.

MEGALODON

This shark is swimming in the deep,
where the ocean floor is steep.
It gives me a creep.
Swim?
I don't dare!
Ocean?
Won't venture into there,
cause I breathe land air.
Trickle, tickle, talk.
I prefer to walk
on a solid dock.
Hunting shark,
in an ocean dark,
far from the sandy shore
would be a deadly chore.
So, I don't want a shark, anymore.

DILOPHOSAURUS

This dino's colors do impress,
I really must confess.
But as you can probably guess,
the rest of him is a mess.
I think that he is crazy!
I think that he's insane.
I'm not even sure,
if he has got a brain!
It kind of makes me frown,
cause I'd like to chase him down.
But, I don't want a clown
to showoff in cave-town.

STEGOSAURUS

I gave a wail,
grabbed him by the tail,
and pulled till I was pale.
But, he dragged me down the trail.
He walked pretty slow.
Still, I let him go
because he had too many spikes,
for my wants or likes.

BRONTOSAURUS

Fee, Fi, Foo,
won't let him go!
Free, fri, frow,
stomped on my toe!
Can't tell a lie,
really did start to cry.
But, I want you to know
I didn't let him go,
till he raised me up so high
I thought I would die!
When I began to scream
he dropped me in a stream.
I will need a team,
to catch this dino dream!

PTERODACTYL

When I threw a rock,
it began to squawk.
Now, this dino is too high,
flying in the sky.
I can only wave, "Bye-bye."

ANKYLOSAURUS

Trap, Tap, Snap.
Caught a dino in a snare,
but how that snare did tear.
Humpy, bumpy, rumpy.
On his backside,
I went for a ride.
The dino wouldn't trot
the way I thought he ought.
I hit him with my stick,
thinking that would do the trick.
Dino answered with his tail,
raining down a beating hail.
I swung with my fist,
but I widely missed.
Oh, how the dino hissed,
"EAT MY CLUB, BUB!"
Then he gave me a pop—
a really hard bop,
on the very tip top
of my head.
I went plop,
and the dino-ride did stop.

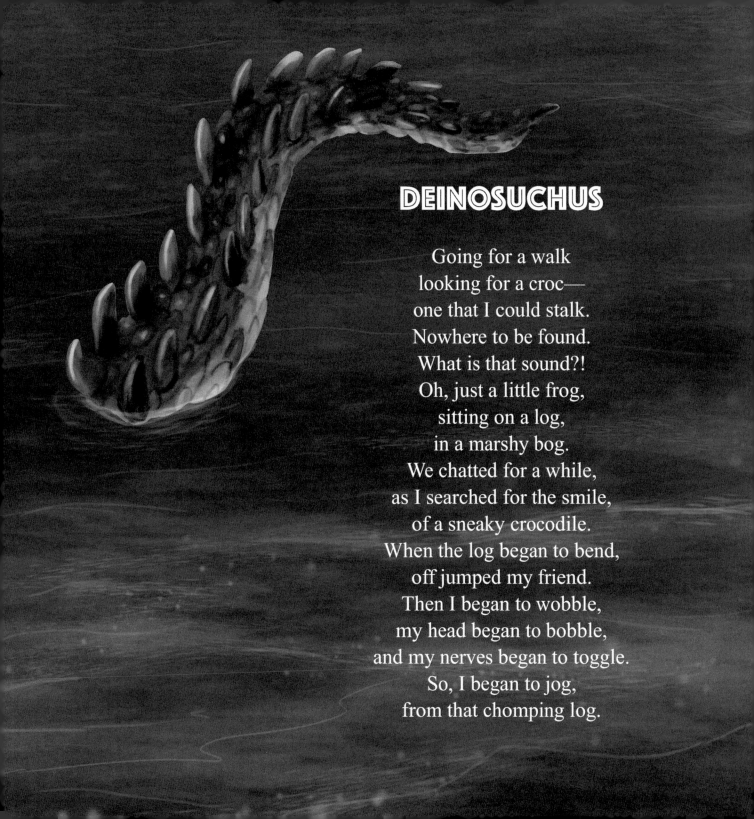

DEINOSUCHUS

Going for a walk
looking for a croc—
one that I could stalk.
Nowhere to be found.
What is that sound?!
Oh, just a little frog,
sitting on a log,
in a marshy bog.
We chatted for a while,
as I searched for the smile,
of a sneaky crocodile.
When the log began to bend,
off jumped my friend.
Then I began to wobble,
my head began to bobble,
and my nerves began to toggle.
So, I began to jog,
from that chomping log.

DIMETRODON

This dino is too pink,
and his breath has got a stink.
It makes my nose want to shrink,
my eyes start to blink,
and really makes me think
I am on the brink...
of throwing up!

TRICERATOPS

Look at this dino,
almost like a rhino.
Has too many horns,
doesn't she?
One, two, three.
That's what I see.
Three too many horns,
for me!
Do you agree?

SABERTOOTH TIGER

Grunt, growl, groan.
Chewing on a bone,
not a lion or a liger,
but a Sabertooth Tiger!
This tiger is too grumpy.
His tail's a little stumpy.
And every time he growls,
he bares salivating jowls.
Paws with claws,
yellow-fanged jaws—
gripping, ripping, saws!
When he made a moan,
I didn't like the tone.
When I heard his tummy rumble,
I felt pretty humble.
My courage did crumble,
and I began to stumble
back, back, back.
Back I did track,
out of his cave,
that would've been my grave,
had I been more brave.

TYRANNOSAURUS

This baby dino is so small,
he'd make the perfect doll.
He is so very cute,
catching him would be a hoot,
if only...
his mama wasn't such a brute.

SPINOSAURUS

With a stomp and a chomp,
T–Rex charged after me!
Then we fell in a swampy sea,
with mud up to the knee.
I struggled to get free;
and was about to croak,
when something worse than Rex, awoke.
Silence broke,
as this new terror spoke,
"Roarrrrr!"

Rex and I froze,
as a giant figure rose,
into the height,
of the moon's bright
white light.
A razor spine glistened,
as a dark monster listened.
The thing that stood before us,
was an angry Spinosaurus!
Scratch, claw, bite!
Rex and he began to fight,
with all their strength and might.
And this I saw, as my invite,
to make sweet flight,
out of sight
into the purple night.

COMPSOGNATHUS

Tricky, ticky, tock,
sleeping on a rock.
Finally I caught,
the dino that I sought.
He wasn't too scary,
or so very hairy,
and was a dino I could carry.
He was pretty lean,
but at least he wasn't mean.
Not a giant beast,
for a large family feast.
Just a tiny little dino,
I think I'll make him mino.

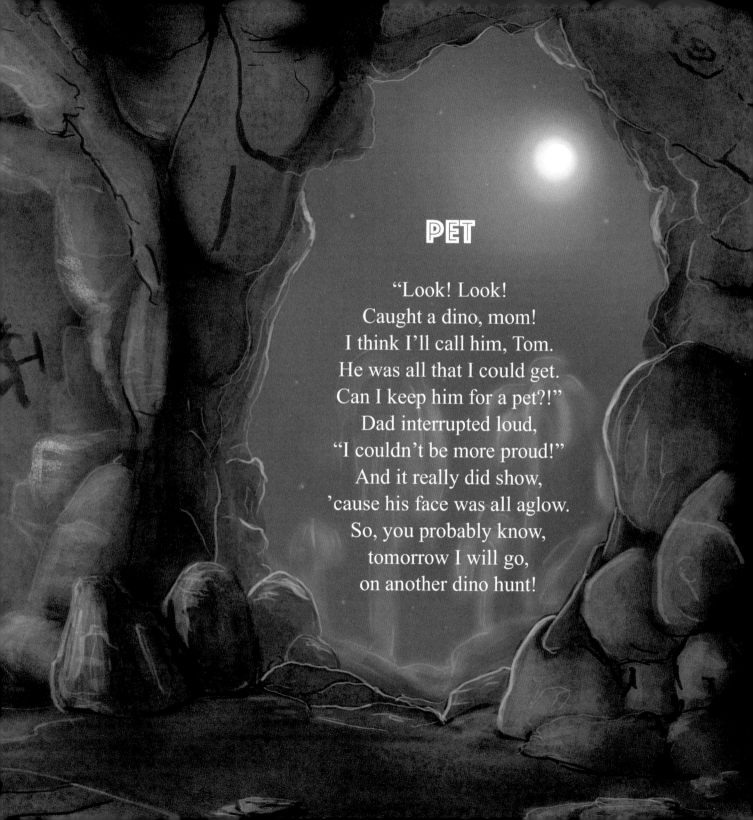

PET

"Look! Look!
Caught a dino, mom!
I think I'll call him, Tom.
He was all that I could get.
Can I keep him for a pet?!"
Dad interrupted loud,
"I couldn't be more proud!"
And it really did show,
'cause his face was all aglow.
So, you probably know,
tomorrow I will go,
on another dino hunt!

DINO DREAMS

Done with your chore?
Time to sleep some more.
Snuggle, Sniffle, Snore.
Sleeping's not a bore,
but a wonderful door
to a dino land of lore,
where the biggest dinosaur
gives a big n' mighty roar,
and the screeching dragons soar
over jungle rains that pour,
—so exciting to explore,
as you hunt the dinosaur!
Beasts they are born,
with a skin of thorn,
a face of horn,
a neck of rail,
a spine of nail,
a tail to impale,
and a belly made of mail.
These dino dreams you adore,
are treasures you will store,
forever a part,
of your little patting heart.
Good night, Jonathan.
We love you.

Made in the USA
Middletown, DE
18 November 2019